Benjamin Franklin Allen

Irene or the Life and Fortunes of a Yankee Girl

A Tale, in Eight Cantos

Benjamin Franklin Allen

Irene or the Life and Fortunes of a Yankee Girl
A Tale, in Eight Cantos

ISBN/EAN: 9783337023225

Printed in Europe, USA, Canada, Australia, Japan

Cover: Foto ©Andreas Hilbeck / pixelio.de

More available books at **www.hansebooks.com**

IRENE

Or, The Life and Fortunes of

A YANKEE GIRL.

A TALE, IN EIGHT CANTOS.

BY

Dr. B. F. ALLEN,
Author of "The Uncle's Legacy," etc.

Labor ipse et voluptas et laudabilis.

JOLIET, ILL.
SIGNAL PRINTING OFFICE.
1878.

TO MY WIFE,

The faithful companion of many years, sharer of my joys and sorrows, who timidly shrinks from any public notoriety, this volume is affectionately inscribed.

PREFACE.

A long preface is an unmitigated outrage. A writer has no business to attempt such an infliction upon a discerning public. To expect that it will be read is presuming too much on human patience. Some persons *never* read a preface, however short. In fact, it is generally a dull, prosy sort of composition, and does not tend much to the enlightenment or edification, and certainly not to the amusement of those who are good-natured enough to wade through it.

With such a knowledge of facts before us, we shall not attempt even a brief synopsis of the following story, because we do not wish our kind readers to get offended with us in the outset, and thereby criticize us with more asperity than we deserve.

High flights of fancy, or sudden and startling poetical imagery, have not been aimed at, but the writer has the vanity to believe that there is a smooth, flowing plainness of verse that may please many readers more, on account of the ease with which the narrative may be perused and understood.

The writer presents very slight claims for *invention* of plot in the following tale. Most of the incidents narrated actually occurred within his own knowledge, while others were suggested by the gossip of the curious.   Though the pronoun I is used freely in the narration, we wish the reader distinctly to understand that it is in no sense of the word an autobiography.

We acknowledge that it is with trembling anxiety that we look forward to the reception of such an unpretending domestic story by a Public which has become so *fast* that nothing short of exciting, improbable "blood and thunder" extravagance will be able to entertain or fill its expectations.   Still we hope there may yet be a sober, sensible few, who will enjoy our efforts.   Trusting therefore to the favor of those few, with fluttering pinions, we take flight into the cloudy, uncertain atmosphere of authorship.

CONTENTS.

PRELUDE.

Come and listen now awhile,
Let our song your cares beguile,
While our trembling harpstrings swell,

And in gentle numbers tell
Of a land both good and fair,
Where the verdant prairies are ;
Where, unchecked, the eye may trace,
Through illimitable space,
Laughing fields of golden grain,
Stretching o'er the extended plain,
And the breeze-skimmed meadows gleaming,
In the bright sun's radiance beaming ;
While the half-grown corn is seen,
With its deeper, richer green,
Not unlike the breast of ocean,
Zephyr kissed, with rippling motion ;
Where the plowman, void of care,
Guides with ease his silver share ;

Where no rocks or stones impede,
When the sower sows his seed ;
Where the laborer's tasks are lighter,
And the summer's sunshine brighter ;
Where the maidens, blither, fairer,
Charm with graces, richer, rarer,
Nobler thoughts their acts impelling,
Warmer love their bosoms swelling,
While our breasts with rapture thrill,
Captive lead our hearts at will !
All we view, with ardor fires,
Kindling in us new desires.

When we take a calm survey
Of the wonders in our way,
View the glories all outspread,
Heaven's bright archway overhead,
All the gladness strewn abroad,
Lifts our souls to Nature's God !

Poets sing of rocks and mountains,
Silvery streams and crystal fountains,

Purling brooks and murmuring rills,
Cascades leaping from the hills,
Sylvan groves and wooded dells,
Glittering spires, and chiming bells,
Gorgeous palaces of old,
Decked with richest gems and gold;
Of the perils of old ocean,
Of the hurricane's commotion,
Of the stormy battle's strife,
Struggling nations wage for life:
Of the daring deeds of heroes,
Or of cruel modern Neros;
Oft of tales and acts that shock us,
Of heroic feats that mock us,
By their very greatness, saying,
We're but dwarfs or pigmies, weighing,
In life's balance, altogether,
Scarce enough to turn a feather.
Prithee, now, inspire my song,
Softer, sweeter strains prolong,

While a happier theme we choose,
Cheer us, aid us, Gentle Muse!
  Not of legends, old and hoary,
Not of warriors, grim and gory,
Nor of heroes famed in story,
But the healthy, active life
Manhood feels, while in the strife,
Struggling 'gainst ill fortune's tides,
Climbing steep the mountain's sides,
In the rugged path of duty,
Winning love and smiles from beauty;
And the subtle, swelling stream,
Playful as a fairy dream,
Welling up from woman's heart,
Sudden touched by love's keen dart;
Of her lasting, true devotion,
Of the lively, sweet commotion,
Stirring in man's sterner breast,
When he yields to love's behest;
To *such* themes my strains belong,
These the burden of my song.

IRENE.

___

CANTO I.

CHILDHOOD TO MANHOOD—WHAT SHALL I DO?

Loved are thy banks, majestic, noble river!

   Through whose broad channel half a hemisphere

Pours forth unmeasured waters, staying never;

   Now, in smooth, gentle current, soft and clear;

Now, surging in wild eddies, varying ever;

   Anon, thy sweeping torrent brings thee near,

And pours thee in the yawning gulf, the cup

From which insatiate ocean drinks thee up.

St. Lawrence! purest, clearest, noblest, best;

 Fond memories of my youth, oft turn to thee;

Near thy bright stream my boyhood days were blest;

 My limbs caught vigor, while in sportive glee,

I plunged within thy waters, with much zest,

 Or poled my slab-raft on thy bosom free.

And later, urged with sturdy oar, the boat,

My hands had fashioned on thy waves to float.

How often have I made, in boyhood's days,

 Sad havoc with the finny tribes that glide

Through thy pure waters; in what varied ways,

 Enticed them to my snares, from thy clear tide,

With worm-hid hook, dropp'd near their lurking place,

 Or while o'er thy fair bosom, swift I'd ride,

My trolling barb, and red, deceptive bait,

With glaring show, oft lured them to their fate.

And, oft, the pitch-pine torchlight, gleaming bright,

    My boat has flashed across thy silvery tide,

When all else by the sable shrouds of night

    Were veil'd in gloom and darkness, thick spread wide;

While trusty comrade, aided by the light,

    With paddle o'er thy bays, my craft would guide;

With anxious eyes, into thy depths I'd peer,

And pierce thy tenants with the deadly spear.

How often have I climbed the rugged steeps

    That skirt thy crystal waters, lovely stream !

Or rambled o'er thy sloping banks, where peeps

    The modest heath plant, fragrant as a dream ;

With fruit so sweet, which in its moss bed sleeps,

    The fabled nectar of the gods would seem

Insipid, when with it compared, I ween,

Delicious, aromatic wintergreen !

There also in the rosy month of June,

   While Sol shed down his ardent mellow rays.

And wild birds warbled forth melodious tune,

   I've passed delightedly the livelong days,

Gathered rich whortleberries, thick bestrewn,

   'Mid tangled, leafy shrubs, their hiding place ;

The nimble squirrel chased, with untold pleasures,

Or robb'd the wild duck's nest to gain her treasures.

Oh, pleasant childhood's scenes, how art thou fled !

   Thy joyful, sweet delights. forever past !

Now, only on the page of memory read ;

   Yet retrospective thoughts delicious cast

Their burdens o'er my senses, while I tread

   Thy flow'ry paths, in fancy's maze, though fast

The hurried moments sweep, and all are gone ;

The real present, stern, remains alone !

     *   *   *   *   *

The plan, or programme, erst that filled my brain,
　　The thoughts revolving there, which made it rife
With strong desire to write, did thus constrain
　　Me to attempt the story of my life.
Yet now I fear the effort will be vain ;
　　For, free from thrilling incident or strife,
My tale will be not wrought in fancy shapes,
Nor 'blood and thunder' scenes. nor hairbreadth 'scapes

A little unproductive farm was all
　　The wealth my honest parents then possessed ;
From this, with strict economy. though small,
　　The avails supplied our real wants. and blessed
With health, reward of those who heed the call
　　To work by day and give their nights to rest ;
From youth to vig'rous manhood grew my frame ;
Yet cramped in intellect, unknown to Fame.

Though long ere this, swelled with desire my soul,

　To burst the bands in sunder that confined

My restless yearnings; and to escape the goal

　Which held enthrall'd, in shorten'd check, my mind.

But none with skill to guide, or to control

　My wayward, struggling fancies, could I find.

And thus, ambition stilled, I scarce know how,

I whistled cheerful as I drove the plow.

In those good, quiet days of long ago,

　When earnest, faithful industry was thought

A virtue, worthy fostering care, and so

　Good parents aim'd to have their children taught;

Obedience and respect were not deemed *slow*;

　And children lived and grew, as if they ought

To give, in all things, without doubt or question,

Good heed to father's counsel or suggestion.

How diff'rent now, with all the means in use,

    To make boys *smart,* or saucy, sharp and *fast;*

Now "Young America," with what abuse,

    The good and sage advice of friends, will cast

Away! when kindly proffered, to induce

    Him to take thought upon the future vast;

Results of conduct, good or ill! The vogue is

To call such friends or parents dull " *Old fogies !* "

Oh, could we to old times again return,

    Those good old days, for which we sigh in vain!

How 'twould relieve poor parents' hearts that burn

    With fond anxiety, and grief, and pain;

Stung by ingratitude! While forced to learn

    That loved and cherished offspring will not deign

To obey, or listen to their counsels meet;

But *morals* learn from *rowdies* in the street!

My father's stock of books was small, indeed :

 A dozen volumes would comprise them all !

No romances or hist'ries there to lead

 The young and ardent intellect, or call

In play the undeveloped powers, or feed

 A starved imagination, though so small ;

Yet Nature's volumes rich, their charms did lend ;

And sometimes books from a congenial friend.

Thus grew I up to manhood, vig'rous, strong ;

 My parents o'er my labors, claimed no more

Control. The years were gone that seemed so long ;

 And *twenty-one !* I stood on life's broad shore,

Ready to launch among the busy throng,

 My untried bark on the rough sea ; or soar

With untrained wings, aerial heights profound ;

Or, failing, fall, to grovel on the ground.

Yes, now I stood on manhood's verge alone,

    And fain the rugged steeps of life would climb;

With empty purse, unhonored and unknown!

    Could I thus hope to mount its heights sublime.

And by unaided effort still atone

    For early culture's lack; redeem the time,

In youth, without improvement, thus passed by?

Succeed or fail, I still resolved to *Try*.

With longing, deep desire, I'd looked for years,

    Through the dim future's vista to this day;

This day, which, to impatient youth, appears,

    In amber colors decked, and bright array;

Sweet, ardent hope, her mighty fabric rears,

    And fairy spirits in her temples play;

Thus, in the distance; yet, when reached, 'twill fall;

A crumbling mass of ruins tells it all!

'Tis now we feel that all the stays and props

    We leaned upon before are knocked aside;

The present, now, the amber curtain drops,

    And rainbow mists are scattered far and wide;

Sudden, the fancy-wove vagary stops;—

    And now, with vision cleared, we quickly glide

Into the spot, where all unveiled, we trace

Life's stern and real conflicts, face to face.

So anxious eaglets, with a wild unrest,

    While half-grown and unfledged, thus long to fly,

Scarce brook control, within the parent nest;

    But eager, ever, their new wings to try,

Would fain launch forth; yet later, when possessed

    With full grown pinions, fit to skim the sky,

Dare not the attempt, so listless grown and coy,

Till parent birds the dear old nest destroy.

Thus like the eaglet, trembling, paused I now,

    Uncertain what to do, or where to turn ;

An earnest *work* forced to pursue, but how ?

    A rugged path, if I would laurels earn ;

No wealthy friend was there, with gold to endow,

    Or help me, then, the world's rough ways to learn;

But struggling all alone, the course I chose

    Another prosy chapter will disclose.

CANTO II.

EFFORT AND EXERTION—AN INCIDENT.

A little, quiet neighborhood that lay

    Imbosomed almost in the forest wild,

From home, some half a dozen miles away,

    Where untaught children grew and peaceful smiled,

Spending bright childhood's hour in idle play,

    Or older grown, beside their parents toiled ;

Desired a teacher, their young steps to guide ;

And to " your humble servant " thus applied.

This happened just as I had reached that age,

    When ready to go forth and leave behind ·

Parents and friends, so glad did I engage,

    For modest pay, to train the youthful mind;

Some to advance from alphabetic page;

    Many, dull, wayward, restless, others kind;—

There, faithful labored I, to fill the station,

And, with success, won patrons' approbation.

But, this employment, humble though it were,

    A few short months was all I could pursue;

The toiling, struggling settlers would not dare

To pay my scanty wages, scarcely through

The winter; and when spring again laid bare

    The smiling earth, to school I bade adieu;

Then turned, with earnest hands, again to toil,

And helped to cultivate the grudging soil.

My honest parents, always kind and good.

Shrined be their mem'ry ever in my heart!

For num'rous offspring furnished clothes and food,

And from their humble means could not impart,

By patrimonial gifts; yet ever stood

Ready to help me in a forward start;

And when returned again to labor hard.

Paid for my work a laborer's full reward.

Incited thus with hope of gain, though long,

The summer months at length had passed away,

And now desire for learning, always strong,

Swell'd in my heart, and strengthen'd day by day.

With hope alluring to be classed among

The wise and good of earth; without delay,

My mind and purpose fixed on gaining knowledge,

I hastened to an academic college.

True, many think of school days with disgust,

    And deem their efforts there a heavy task;

They enter classic halls because they must.

    And not because they choose, or love to bask

In learning's glorious light; but place their trust

    In *keys* or *poneys*, striving thus to mask

Their ignorance, until they may ride through;

But vain the veil; 'tis ever plain to view.

With me not thus.   With eager joy I went

    Within those honored halls, my mind to improve :

Thus is it ever; and, with strong intent,

    We seek with rapture, little short of love,

And with much energy our minds are bent

    On what of good is placed almost above

Our reach; yet, when with ease it falls, we turn,

And oft with loathing, proffered blessings spurn.

Here I could feast the cravings of my soul
  With books, and teachers competent to give
Instruction needed, and my mind control;
  And in continued revel did it live,
Imbibing precious drink from Learning's bowl;
  Expanding with each draught it did receive;
Till, while thus drinking, it would almost seem
The waters had been drawn from Lethe's stream.[1]

As thought reverts to those enchanting days,
  With what sweet mem'ry still my soul is thrilled;
There, in life's desert wand'rings was *one* place
  Where crystal fountains, sparkling waters filled;
And herbage green veiled Nature's lovely face;
  Where beauteous birds melodious music trilled,
And so entranced the mind, shut out all care,
That life's dull, heavy load seemed cast off there.

But soon, ah soon, this precious charm was broke!

    Life, its stern conflicts soon renewed again;

From this sweet dream, compelled, I soon awoke;

    Efforts to shun the battle all were vain;

No strategy might check or turn the stroke;

    For, vanished as the snow by sudden rain,

My hard earned pittance had dissolved in air,

And work, *hard* work, must now the loss repair.

For gold I cared not; that is, for itself,

    And only valued what the gold would buy;

And, but for that, quite idle on the shelf,

    It might remain without my asking why,

Esteemed as naught but worthless, paltry pelf.

    Yet now, when learning's paths I fain would try,

I could not without gold much wisdom bring,

By just a wish, as once did Israel's king.

And thus again for wages must I strive,

   With which more hidden knowledge might be bought

And stimulate the fires that kept alive

   The kindling rays that would illumine thought;

And from no other source could I derive

   So well the means desired, as when was taught

Within the little humble house that stood,

The country school, imbosomed in the wood.

So to another school I did repair,

   Of somewhat more pretentions than the other,

Requiring more of labor, skill and care;

   Again achieved success, without much pother.

" Delightful task the *tender* thought to rear,"—

   (Not quite so easy *tougher* ones to smother)—

'Tis plain the one who wrote thus, though no fool,

Had never taught a country district school.

But, if this school more labor did require,

    It also yielded greater compensation,

Which, with my increased knowledge, did inspire

    With greater zeal to fill the situation;

And as my aim was still to mount up higher,

    And occupy a more exalted station,

Toil and privation, patient I endured,

That thus the wished for boon might be secured.

And thus through half a dozen years or more,

    I spent the time teaching or being taught,

And yet my means were slender as before,

    Still, the past years had not been spent for nought;

The cost I'd gained in learning's precious store,

    Nor deem'd the knowledge thus too dearly bought.

But now 'twas time to seek, besides enjoyment.

Some occupation for a life employment.

     *   *   *   *   *

Once, ere this time, burst sudden on my sight
    A witching vision of sweet loveliness;
A form more graceful, or a face more bright,
    Seemed never lent from Heaven mankind to bless.
Her eyes of hazel beamed a mellow light,
    And glossy ringlets 'scaped confining tress,
Wildly luxuriant in the soft breeze played,
Shading her lovely neck and shoulders, strayed.

Whene'er her sweet voice warbled forth in song,
    Or trancing smile, her ruby lips did part;
The dulcet tones, soft echoes would prolong,
    And mem'ries of that smile, around the heart,
Would linger ever, claiming place among
    The sweetest recollections; though no art,
To fashion's rule, had ever " trained her pace,"
    Her step so light all art excelled in grace.

She'd lost her way; and like a frightened bird,

    No more, unaided, could the path regain;

In sweet, yet trembling accents, breathed the wor(

    That told she sought her absent friends in vain.

A chaste and hallowed thought my being stirred—

    A case of " first sight love." 'twas very plain—

So, gladly the assistance wished, I gave her,

Well pleased that I might grant her such a favor.

Had she been old and ugly, grim and gaunt,

    And void of charms, a female in distress,

Appealing thus for aid, I glad would grant

    The assistance in my power, e'en though her dres

Might be of coarser stuff; yet still I can't

    Assert, in such a case, that I should press

My efforts to the task, e'en though 'twere duty,

So eager as for loveliness and beauty.

A hearty, kind regard I always had

    For womankind; a woman was my mother;

And since my first remembrance, when a lad

    At district school, I always did much rather

Find place in class beside some pretty maid;

    Kind sisters also owned me as a brother;

Yet never had my heart been captured quite,

Till o'er it flashed this vision, lovely, bright.

To other eyes, perhaps, the world might hold

    Thousands of beings as divine as she,

But, if to others' view it might unfold

    Perfections infinite, 'twas nought to me.

If matches are heaven-made, as has been told.

    And somewhere each has his " *affinity*,"

I had, I felt within my inmost heart,

Of the world's " scissors," met the other part.[2]

Oh, could I then have claimed her for my own,

How blest on earth had been my happy lot!

The worth of wealth till now I ne'er had known;—

But house, or wealth. or fortune I had not;

And though from that pure face, resplendent shone

The light of love returned, yet prudence taught,

Despite my heart's desire, I might not dare

To ask her love my poverty to share.

Yet then I pledged her that some future day,

When wealth or competence I might possess—

Would she agree in maidenhood to stay,

And then my happy soul in union bless—

I'd seek her through the world, while hope a ray

Of light might shed to guide me to the place

Where she should dwell; she readily assented,

And both, that we so soon must part, lamented.

So, with her friends, again she journeyed on,

And, like a meteor, vanished from my sight;—
'Mongst all the world, I felt myself alone,

As if the darkling clouds had veiled the light,
Or that the sun which once so brightly shone,

Had sunk beneath the gloom of sudden night.
Yet from my thoughts, sweet mem'ries of that face,
Time, with its changes, never could displace.

So, when night's silken curtains have o'erspread

The world, and mortals all are hushed in sleep,
In fancy, through elysian fields we're led,

And sweet, delicious dreams our senses keep;
But when bright morn on earth her light has shed,

Again we're wakened from our slumbers deep;
Our pleasing visions soon are gone, we find,
And nought but grateful mem'ries left behind.

I pondered long, and sought kind friend's advice,

　　Whether to learn the law, or healing art;

Some urged me to the first, and looked quite wise,

　　Some thought to cure life's ills the better part;

But, at this time, "the pearl of great price,"

　　I'd not secured, or met "a change of heart;"

And though I'd always found success as teacher,

None ever deemed me fit to make a preacher.

Then half my mind was formed to try the first;

　　I thought my talent lay in that direction;

The germs of eloquence, if kindly nursed,

　　Might win me wealth and fame; yet due reflection

Convinced me lawyer's morals were the worst,[3]

　　And this, alone, formed infinite objection;

For, better poor remain, with conscience healthy,

Than, by dishonest practice, grow more wealthy.

So, to a doctor's shop did I repair,

 And o'er his old, scholastic volumes pored,

For three long years, with anxious, studious care,

 With formulas and maxims, mem'ry stored;

And more advanced, did oft his practice share,

 Gave pills and powders, while ambition soared,

And kept my mind intent on gaining knowledge,

Till off I went to attend a doctor's college.

Here, for some months, my poor bewildered brain

 Was crammed, *ad nauseam*, till more than filled

With symptoms, diagnoses, aches and pains;

 And oft my sympathizing senses chilled,

With horrid shrieks and groans, and efforts vain

 To escape, of suffering victims, firmly held,

Tortured, while skilled professors, high in station,

Performed some murd'rous cutting operation.

Day after day they gave us learned discourse,

     How fleshly ills with potions we might cure;

Talked wise of blood and bile, and other source

     Whence spring the maladies we oft endure;

Told of their wondrous healing deeds, of course;

     Whispered how tact and manner would secure,

In all our future practice much success,

And how, with health restored, mankind to bless.

From this learned college I emerged at last,

     And, having *read* the time the laws require,

Supposed the trying ordeal wholly past,

     And won the goal to which hope did aspire;

Yet now to find a place, in field so vast,

     For future labor. was my great desire;

But how or where, was still a hidden mystery;

So, turn we now to *others* in this history.

CANTO III.

A NEW ENGLAND HOME—THE HEROINE.

In a sweet vale, amongst the hills,

Nursed by the sparkling mountain rills,

Where runs its tortuous course between

A double fringe of willows green,

Or, in its rugged banks confined,

With fir, pine, spruce and hemlock lined ;

Sometimes, o'er pebbles, soft and slow,

In gentle murmuring currents' flow,

Anon, in surging torrent wild,

O'er jagged rocks, by nature piled,

As if to check its headstrong will,

And force its power to turn the mill,

A silvery stream, soft, pure and clear,

In wanton pride, meanders here.

When the bright sun with fervor glows,

And breathes upon the wintry snows,

His ardent breath so swells the tide

Of rills adown the mountain side,

Mingled with spring's dissolving rains,

The swollen flood such volume gains,

With rushing force and wild turmoil,

Made turbid by alluvial soil,

That timber raft or laden boat

Will lightly o'er its bosom float;

Its waters, broad and deep, would seem

The channel of a mighty stream,—

With aspect neither mild nor tame;

In *fact* a *river* as in name.

But when midsummer's thirsty rays

Descend in scorching, fiery blaze,

The surplus waters soon are drunk

Up, or into the parched earth sunk,—

Then, shrunk in size, 'twould scarcely seem

A river, but a rippling stream,—

A footman might its current wade ;

Or cattle seek the cooling shade

It banks give forth, and, half awake,

Stand, in the stream, their thirst to slake ;

The goading flies. brush from their sides,

That pierce and sting their thick tough hides ;

Or, for scant, tender herbs explore

The tangled shrubs that skirt the shore.

   Along the indented margin lay

Sometimes an inlet, cove or bay,

Where alder, birch and hemlock green

Lie mirrored bright, in emerald sheen ;

Where webbed-foot, feathered tribes abide,

And, with swift paddle strokes, divide

The crystal flood, and o'er it glide;

Or, on its placid bosom rest,

Light as the feathery mountain mist.

Securely hid, the mottled trout,

Keen from his rocky bed looks out,

And, darting through the crystal light,

Snaps luckless flies that meet his sight;

And, lured by some attractive bait,

With greedy haste oft seals his fate;

Enticed to seize the treach'rous hook,

Becomes a morsel for the cook,

And, pampered epicures declare,

Nought can excel the dainty fare.

So we the alluring baits of sin,

Oft swallow down, nor see within,

The hidden barb, so eager sought,

Till by its shaft securely caught.

The river's banks, for some extent,

Slope in a gradual, smooth ascent;

But, further back, in lofty sweeps,

High, rockbound hills, from rugged steeps,

Look down along the vale below,

And watch the gentle river's flow;

Like giant sentinels 'twould seem,

The guardians of this mountain stream.

Here, ages past, by earthquake shock,

Cleft and upheaved, the granite rock

Had formed within a lovely grot,

Nearly where rears a farmer's cot,

That nestles in the sylvan shade,

By poplar, larch and cedar spread.

Here, years agone, had made their lair,

The prowling wolf or shaggy bear;

Long ere the woodman's axe had laid

The giant oaks in forest glade;

Long ere the white man's farms were clear'd,

Or white man's dwellings had been reared.

Should any reader care to know

Whether my song be false or true,

Whether the spot I've tried to paint,

Perhaps in colors dull and faint,

Exists, without exaggeration,

Or only in imagination,

To keep such querying thoughts at ease,

(An author's aim should be to please,)

I'll give, in brief, the true location

Of objects named in this relation.

That all may understand my tale,

Know, then, this pictured, lovely vale,

You, in New Hampshire may discover;

And Amonoosuc is the river.

The forest's giants now were felled,

The soil by sturdy plowmen tilled,

The wild beasts had their lair forsook,

To deeper shades themselves betook;

And, of his hunting grounds bereft,

" Lo! the poor Indian," too, had left.

This Indian, whom the poets sing,

So nobly proud, the forest's king!

This Indian, artful, cunning, sly,

With panther's step and eagle's eye,

Who, for long years, his thoughts amused,

And friendship's sacred rights abused,

By prowling 'round the white man's dwelling,

And oft, with demon's war-whoop yelling,

Concealed by midnight's pitchy dark,

Entered, and left an Indian's mark!

The father, hushed in final sleep,

By tomahawk's fell, lightning sweep!
The tender infant's wail or scream,
Stilled by a dash against the beam!
The frantic mother captive led,
Within the wildwood's deepest shade,
And kept on scant starvation's fare,
Till ling'ring death answered her prayer!
This crafty, treach'rous, savage *thing*,
This genuine Indian I would sing,
Who'd fled, like a dissolving dream,
From Amonoosuc's peaceful stream.

No more with fear the timid quake,
Nor hideous whoop their slumbers break!
The " pale face " has dominion now
Obtained, no matter when or how.
Serene along this fertile vale,
The arts of peace alone prevail.

Within the cottage I've portrayed,

Shut close within the greenwood's shade,

On all sides spread his little farm.

Sheltered secure from mountain storm ;

Washed by the river's rippling wave,

And near the rocky hillside cave,

Here peaceful dwelt, inured to toil,

An honest tiller of the soil ;

With his kind wife, a noble pair,

And num'rous offspring young and fair,

Bright objects of their love and care.

Though not indued with sumptuous wealth,

Gleamed ev'ry brow with rosy health,

Of cheerful active life, the fruit,

Sure as the branch from budding shoot.

The father toiled with vig'rous hand,

To force rich products from his land ;

Yet, though unwearied efforts made,

Not generous yield his toil repaid ;

For, narrow was the vale confined,

'Twixt river front and hills behind,

Which, thick o'erspread with granite rocks,

Gave scanty pasture for his flocks ;

Nor opening furrow could divide

The hardened soil on mountain side.

    The mother, too, with restless hands,

Performed what household care demands ;

Plied needle, loom or spinning wheel,

Nor scorned to arrange the frugal meal,

Watched carefully her children's graces,

Expanding forms and winsome faces ;

Trained them in paths of virtue true,

.While industry was kept in view ;

And, day by day, some stent or task,

Not hard to be performed, would ask

From each; when done, they off to school,

By universal Yankee rule,

Were sent, hidden myst'ries to explore,

And tiresome school books' page scan o'er.

But district schools have long vacations,

Sometimes e'en longer than their sessions,

And then, when morning tasks were wrought,

New beauty, health and life they caught

From the pure breath of mountain air,

That lingered in the valley fair,

And blithely kissing, left rich showers

Of stolen sweets from balmy flowers

On brow and cheek; while every pace,

To their lithe forms, lent artless grace;

While strolling 'long the river side,

Or laving in its shallow tide;

Or culling wild flowers, oft that peep

Along the hillside's rugged steep;

Or in the garden scattered seeds

Of choice flowers, and plucked the weeds

That choked their growth; their branches trained,

With hands not idle. soiled and stained;

Or roamed to search in wooded plain

For luscious berries; not in vain,

As, when returned, the purple glow,

On tell-tale lips and fingers show.

And when the autumn's frosted breeze

Had dashed the brown nuts from the trees,

Like wild gazelles, with nimble feet,

Hied forth, the early morn to greet;

With baskets, satchels, sacks or measures,

Secured the forest's dainty treasures.

Sometimes, with patience long drawn out,

They angled for the dainty trout;

And though their spoils were rare and few,

Coursed through their veins, in currents new,

The warm and glowing active life,

Deep'ning on brow and cheek so rife,

And, at each quick'ning pulse's start,

Fresh strength and beauty did impart.

Oft when oppressed by noontide heat,

The little wearied maids, retreat

Sought in the rockbound hillside cave,

Whose sheltering walls cool refuge gave;

There rearranged their china dishes,

According to new whims or wishes;

Or, on their mossy couch reclined,

Or, wreathes from leaves and wild flow'rs twined,

To mingle with their shining tresses,

And deck anew their charms and graces;

Or feast their budding, opening senses,

On fascinating love romances;

For maids to these will gain admission

In spite of mother's prohibition.

Thus lived they, blithe and active grown,

Nor pungent sorrow e'er had known.

While all were lovely, good and fair,

The eldest's beauty was more rare—

While all pleased by their charming ways,

Her ev'ry act, intenser grace.

This maid more fully will engage

My pen, and fill my record's page;

To her my noblest strains belong,

Irene, the heroine of my song.

Then wake, my muse divine, and bring

A softer cadence, while I sing!

To dulcet accents, tune my lyre,

And help me breathe poetic fire!

In thoughts that swell, in glowing stream,

A song that's worthy of my theme.

In all the vale, or country 'round,

Where comely damsels most abound,

In all the vale, this lovely maid,

Most beauty, virtue, sense displayed.

Just at that sweet, uncertain verge,

When blooming flowers from buds emerge;

No longer child, yet scarcely woman,

But just that age when all that's human

In girls, becomes a concentration,

To tax our ardent admiration.

The Douglas' daughter, limned by Scott,

With her most winning charms, had not

(When all her artless grace did bring

Such potent spell o'er Scotland's king,)

More power to chain the heart, when seen,

Than this same witching sweet Irene.

No wonder that her slightest smile

Would cares of lovelorn swains beguile ;

No wonder that her slightest frown

Their cup of happiness dashed down !

Nor is it strange that many, fired

With new-found love, her smiles desired !

Yet, while she toyed with hearts at will,

Her own was all unwounded still.

CANTO IV.

MOVING WEST—AN INCIDENT OF THE JOURNEY— ILLINOIS.

Along the Amonoosuc's vale,

Borne on the wings of western gale,

News of a fruitful, fertile land,

Stretched in the distance, far beyond

What had been deemed the utmost bound

Of the rich prize the pilgrims found;

With legends mingled, strange and thrilling.

Came, with a marv'lous wonder, filling

The honest, toiling Yankees' thought,

Made restless, till this land was sought.

'Twas told, this smooth, rich country lay

More than a thousand miles away,

A boundless tract spread far and wide,

Near Mississippi's surging tide,

The teeming soil would millions feed,

The lengthened furrows nought impede;

The prowling Indians all had gone

Still farther toward the setting sun,

And peaceful white man might enjoy

The fruitful lands of Illinois.

This land might be by all obtained,

Who had a trifling pittance gained;

If not, they still might buy the soil.

Who'd strength and purpose meet for toil;

So small the cost, who had the will,

Might own the farm he wished to till.

When sturdy, hale New England heard

These tales, a wild ambition stirred

Their souls, and ev'ry pulses' stroke

Nerved sinewy arms to stubborn oak.

Men, who for years had faithful wrought,

Yet, quite in vain for wealth had sought,

The rockbound, hardened hills among,

And labored early, late and long;

Indulged not oft in dainty fare,

But dwelt with utmost frugal care;

Men, who had breasted time's rude shocks,

Till silvery threads adorned their locks;

And striplings just to manhood sprung,

The old. the middle-aged and young;

(The stimulating. glowing fire

Burning in each a strong desire;)

Marshalled, in many a social band,

Thronged to possess the goodly land.

As, when by Egypt's king oppressed,

The hosts of Israel knew no rest,

Compelled by force to labor hard,

With homely fare and scant reward,

A numerous crowd resolved to go

To lands where milk and honey flow;

With glowing hopes, the march begun,

Marshalled by Amram's favored son,

Pressed onward till the prize was won.

So feathered denizens of the north,

When winter's snows enshroud the earth,

And streams and lakes are locked with ice,

Of needed food find scant supplies,

Go forth in flocks, on wings sublime,

To dwell in some more genial clime.

The lovely valley I've portrayed,

Where dwelt this graceful, blooming maid,

'Mong maidens comely, fair and tall,

The dearest, loveliest of them all;

Sent forth, on pilgrimage, full share,

Its stalwart sons and daughters fair;

Our heroine's father 'mongst the rest,

Sold homestead farm, and journeyed west.

A ponderous wagon covered o'er

With storm-proof tent cloth strong, and four

Most powerful chargers, to propel

The same o'er moorland, hill and dell,

With his loved wife and children fair,

Most worthy objects of his care,

And few choice household goods beside,

Thus took their tedious, toilsome ride.

   The steam horse's track not yet was laid,

Nor hill tops levelled down to "grade;"

Slow was the pace at which they went,

While straining up the steep ascent;

While slack'ning down to vales below,

Checked by the brakes, 'twas likewise slow.

   When night o'ertook and forced their stay,

From inn or dwelling far away,

Beneath the leafy, wooded shade,

Their tented wagon refuge made;

Their faithful, wearied steeds were led

Aside, secured and kindly fed;

The gathered brushwood piled beside

A stump or tree, and match applied;

Bright water, from the spring or rill,

Would soon the pendent kettle fill;

Food from the wagon chest, with care,

Apt, willing hands would quick prepare

A sweet repast, the dainty fare,

An epicure would gladly share.

Oft, ere to sleep had sunk the sun,

Or twilight shadows had begun

To creep o'er valley, hill or stream,

They'd halt to rest their jaded team.

Sometimes the lithe and active maids,

With sympathy for laboring steeds,

For lengthened miles forebore to ride,

But tripped with supple feet beside;

And oft from beaten track would stray,

To cull the wild flowers, near the way;

Or berries seek in wooded glade,

Or nuts within the hazel shade.

The tender-hearted, kind Irene,

With sympathies more quick and keen,

Grieved to behold inflicted pain,

On suffering beasts that can't complain;

And thus to light the heavy load,

Would often walk while others rode.

Once, on a bright sweet autumn day,

O'er earth the lengthened shadows lay,

The sun, low in Heaven's archway hung,

Still cast his struggling rays among

The stinted shrubs in copsewood grown,

And gentle, kind Irene, alone,

Had wandered on, from beaten track,

A path, she hoped might lead her back;

Believed the course her passage lay,

Would verge into the travelled way;

But hastening on, with quickened tread,

The denser thicket shades o'erspread,

Almost shut out the ling'ring rays.

Shed by the sun's departing blaze ;

Her soul chilled, with a sudden frost,

Now conscious that her way was lost ;

When, issuing from the closer wood,

A stranger form before her stood!

His frame was cast in manly mold,

Which youthful maids not loath behold ;

A glance might worth and goodness trace,

In every line that marked his face,

And in his eye resplendent shone

Fidelity and truth alone.

He stood as if spell-bound, amazed,

And on the lovely vision gazed ;

For quickened pace and slight alarm

Lent heightened grace to every charm.

The maiden paused, at glimpse of thought,
Half turned, as if to fly the spot;
But ventured once to meet his look,
When all of fear her mind forsook.

So turns and springs the timid hare,
So stops to see if danger's near.

So, startled bird, with quick affright,
Might spread her wings for sudden flight;
So, reassured, again alight.

The stranger spoke : " I well believe
This Heaven-sent visit I receive,
By some kind chance, my soul to cheer,
And not thy will hath brought thee here.
Say what propitious fate hath led
Thee to this wild, sequestered shade ?"

Listened the maid, and eager heard

Respectful speech in every word,

Read deference in each gentle tone,

And with sweet trust, replied : " Alone,

I sought relief to burdened team

My father drives, nor did I deem

The sylvan footpath I pursued,

Diverged so far from beaten road ;

But now, like ship when tempest tost,

My course and pathway all are lost ;

Yet pray, kind sir, respect my need,

And to my friends my footsteps lead,

For every act of thine compels

Belief that with thee honor dwells."

Glad heard the stranger this request,

And quickened life glowed in his breast ;

Thanked Heaven this lovely maid was sent

To crave a boon he'd power to grant ;

Again found speech : " Fair maid, I must

E'en now give praise for this thy trust.

I know the intricate profound

Of every spot this region 'round,

Yet now 'twere far to follow back

This path, to seek the highroad track ;

But follow on, short space before,

'Twill lead us to the river's shore,

Where snugly moored the bank beside,

A boat will bear us o'er the tide,

Close to a spot not far away,

Where public road winds near the bay ;

There, if we haste, methinks we'll meet

The friends, will glad your presence greet."

    Instinctive fear or sudden dread

Rushed through the bosom of the maid,

For ne'er had she been carried o'er

Deep waters in frail craft before.

Yet, though she felt a wild unrest,

Her fear was smothered in her breast,

And, in her strait, she knew she must,

In boat and guide, place all her trust;

So, gently bade him lead the way,

Along the path where ready lay

The skiff might bear them o'er the bay.

Adown the bank they quickly hied;

He brought the loosed craft close beside

The pebbly beach, then placed within

His tim'rous, shrinking charge, Irene;

Breathed soothing word that might restore

Her hope; stepped in and pushed from shore.

    The sturdy oar the stranger plied,

And shot, like lightning, o'er the tide,

The tiny craft; its graceful weight

Bore, proud of such delicious freight.

At every lengthened stroke he'd bring,

'Twould lightly from the water spring,

Then, settling down, so firm would rest,

The maiden's doubts were all suppressed.

The stranger youth she must admire,

And glowed within her soul new fire;

Her gentle bosom 'gan to move,

Swelled with desire akin to love;

And ere was gained the distance half,

Rung o'er the bay her silvery laugh,

For fear and doubt had fled her breast,

And artless mirth, no more repressed,

The treasured fountain did outfling,

Like sparkling rills from bubbling spring.

Urged by her guide, the maiden sung

In sweetest strains. The stranger hung,

Enraptured, on each thrilling note

That warbled from her mellow throat;

While rocky banks would fain prolong

The swelling accents of her song.

The stranger's voice was also heard,

Blending in full harmonic chord.

Yet not in song was wholly spent

The precious time; sweet converse lent

To blend their hearts, its pure oblation,

And heightened mutual admiration.

_While o'er the crystal bay they glide,

Each to the other did confide

The hist'ry of their earlier years,

Their future plans, their hopes and fears,

And mutual love, their breasts concealed,

By treach'rous eyes was all revealed;

And ere the farther shore was gained,

With thoughts and feelings unrestrained,

Breathed their regard; the plighted word,

Nought but the twilight zephyr heard.

Just as the boat had reached the strand,

They saw the tented wagon stand,

O'erhanging leafy boughs, beneath,

Encircled as in fairy wreath,

Short space beyond, near by the road;

The maiden's heart in transport glowed,

She turned to thank her stranger guide,

For safe transmission o'er the tide;

And, as he viewed the charming grace

Reflected from her upturned face,

Could not forbear one sweet embrace;

He strained her to his manly breast,

And, on half willing lips impressed

One ardent, loving, ling'ring kiss,

Sweet height of raptured human bliss!

The deep'ning twilight shadows spread

Thick mantle o'er the earth. He led

To anxious friends the blushing maid,

Who spoke: " The treacherous path betrayed

Me into tangled thicket shade,

Where, fearing, doubting, lost, dismayed,

This generous stranger I descried,

Who kindly did my footsteps guide

Along the river bank, where lay

His boat; then rowed me o'er the bay."

In earnest, glowing, heartfelt word,

The parents' thanks the stranger heard,

And Heaven's choice blessings on his head,

Then, ere he took departure, said :

" No credit, thanks, or praise is due,

But duty's path did I pursue ;

Yet, if you will such act regard

As claiming merit or reward,

Still burdened debt on me is laid;

Your lovely daughter's smiles repaid,

A thousand times, the effort made.

But now I may no longer dwell,

Except to speak a kind farewell.

Yon shining orb, proud queen of night,

Will o'er the bay my passage light;

Again we'll meet some future day,"

He said; and took his homeward way.

The stranger did so well his part,

As won him place in every heart;

His noble bearing, frank and true,

From all claimed admiration due;

Yet deeper, in Irene's pure breast,

His image, close enshrined, found rest.

She watched the boat recede from shore,

As swift it skimmed the inlet o'er,

Till from her vision all it swept,

And moonlight on the waters slept.

The splash of oars no more was heard,

Nor echoed sound the stillness stirred.

Her swelling bosom heaved a sigh ;

A tear bedimmed her moistened eye ;

She sought her couch by sister's side,

And met in dreams her stranger guide !

———

They journeyed on their toilsome way,

From early morn till twilight gray ;

Climbed o'er the hills and rugged steeps,

Or waded swamps' and marshes' deeps ;

Or stemmed the swollen streamlets' flood,

Whose turbid channels crossed the road ;

Till chill November earth o'erspread,

And opening Heaven its torrents shed ;

While the drenched soil did soft'ning feel,

And mortar clogged the advancing wheel :

Till just before the wintry cloud

Enveloped earth in chilling shroud,

The important object was attained ;

The long sought Illinois-land gained.

There shelt'ring dwelling was secured,

And rest from travel toil assured.

Then turn we now and yield the place

To others, and their hist'ries trace.

CANTO V.

MORE EMIGRATION—THE CAUSES—OCCUPATION.

In older states, where mortal ills

Were few, and num'rous doctors' mills,

Full manned with high professors, were

Fast grinding out, from year to year,

M. D.'s, new grists, on every hand,

Which, scattered broadcast o'er the land.

In every town their stations took,

Or village, cross-roads, corner, nook,

With visage grave, and bustling air,

Dispensed pills, powders, potions, rare;

Rode through the streets with frantic pace,

As if life's thread hung on the race;

Or waited in their dens quite through

The tedious days, with nought to do,

Except to count the swelling bills

Incurred to ward off hunger's chills;

In fact, so numerous were their faces,

They crowded all the opening places;

And if on earth spot might be found,

Where doctors' shops did not abound,

To dullest mind, it was quite clear,

That point was not located here.

So, if I would a harvest share,

To other fields must needs repair ;

Where maladies were oftener met,

And doctors not so plenty yet.

    The great and fertile West, 'twas said,

For years was scourged with plague so dread,

The timid prudent did not dare,

For sake of gain to venture there.

Such cheerless stories had been told,

Yet not believed by all; the bold

And daring sought adventures new,

In spite of woful tales ; if true,

And risk or hazard were incurred,

Physicians should not be deterred.

So, when was done my reading course,

And clinched with college lectures' force.

I felt quite competent to engage,

And 'gainst life's ills a warfare wage.

My greatest want was now the field,

My burnished weapons where to wield;

But yielded to the great demand,

Of the miasmal prairie land.

Another wish, breathed not in voice,

Inducement lent to fix my choice;

Inspiring hope, deep in my breast,

Hid, all enshrined, there let it rest!

Yet, ere my story all is told,

This hidden motive, 'twill unfold.

My brother, who with earnest toil,

In vain had tilled the sterile soil,

And wealth, by sad experience, found

He could not draw from barren ground,

Where spruce and hemlock most abound,

Had lately met a maiden fair,

Life's joys and ills with him to share;

And ere was clasped the nuptial band,

They pledged to seek, in other land,

That wealth denied them here; and blest

With hope, resolved to journey West.

Not yet was laid the steam-horse's track,

And travel, in the old stage hack,

Or overland, by wagon team,

Was tedious, to the last extreme.

E'en steamships, on the lakes were rare,

And quite exorbitant in fare;

But numerous craft, with sailing rig,

Sloop, schooner, frigate, barque, or brig,

At less expense, would bear us o'er

The billowy tide, to destined shore.

On one of these, new, staunch and trim,

Full manned with sailors, dark and grim,

We bade farewell to friends most kind,

And left our childhood's scenes behind,

While smiling hope our fancies cheered,

And vision'd, future fabrics reared.

In blooming springtime, lovely May,

Our good ship cleared from Sackett's bay,

And coursing westward, proud did ride,

O'er old Ontario's troubled tide.

Like mist, borne on by tempest's sweep,

She seemed to skim the mighty deep,

And while the breeze was fair and strong,

Our destined passage seemed not long ;

But, ere our ship much distance sped,

Such airy hopes and visions fled.

'Twere long to tell what checked our speed,

Or onward progress did impede;

How adverse tempests drove us back,

Or forced our vessel oft to tack;

And what disasters dire befell,

While struggling through the great canal;

How closely wedged, in timber locks,

Compelled to back, and hew the blocks,

When hawser felt its utmost strain

To drag us through, yet all in vain;

And how our captain ill could bear

Such obstacles; and dark despair

So all possessed his shattered mind,

He sought in death relief to find;

And in the wildwood, deep and dank,

The moistened soil his life-blood drank!

While suicidal hand was found

To clutch the steel that wrought the wound!

And how much more delay we endured,

While other captain was procured ; [4]

How many days no distance gained,

While " *Eolus* " the winds enchained ;

Like " Ancient Mariner's " ship, not stirred,

Because he shot the ominous bird ;

So we, impatient, days abode,

While ship becalmed, at anchor rode.

Yet transient, all things earthly tend,

But patient wait, to have an end ;

And so our journey, too, begun

Long weeks before, at length was done ;

Our ship, so baffled and detained,

Chicago's port at last had gained ;

While voyagers, a grateful band,

Now reached the long sought prairie land.

    'Tis scarcely worth my while to tell

What scenes and incidents befell

Us, travelling inland, farther west,

O'er prairies rich in verdure dressed;

What vast fields ripe with golden wheat,

On all sides did our vision greet;

What boundless seas of waving corn,

The varying landscape did adorn;

Or how the unbroken prairie teemed

With flowers, that in the sunshine gleamed.

To dwellers in the mighty west,

Whereon such scenes the eye may rest

At will, what seems of little price,

To us then seemed a paradise.

With unsophisticated gaze,

We scanned the wonders with amaze;

The clouds of grouse that beat the air

With whirring wings, we viewed with care;

The flocks of quail, so plump and sly,

We thought the grouse's progeny ;

Till, in their chase our limbs bestirred,

When soon we found them older birds.

Our noble, worthy, trusty steeds,

Stood firm and faithful in our needs ;

The wagon hauled o'er softened soil,

With most unwonted lab'ring toil ;

With strain redoubled, lugged us through

The viscid mire of unbridged slough ;

And when we came the bank beside,

Of swollen stream, or river's tide,

Plunged fearless in and brought us o'er,

Till safely gained the other shore ;

Though pressed by torrent's force to swim,

Yet faltered not in will or limb.

But " *Blackberry* "[5] their utmost powers,

Put to the test ; for recent showers

Had swelled the dark and muddy stream,

And perilous did the passage seem .

Where flood had late the bridge uptorn,

And down the tide its timbers borne ;

And gullied channels worn anew,

Which thickened waters hid from view.

By much success though grown quite bold,

We paused and pondered here, till told,

That, through the fields, just down below,

The distance of a mile or so,

Beyond where flags and rushes lined

The marshy shore, we there might find

A crossing, with less danger fraught ;

We followed down, the passage sought ;

Our steeds dashed in and gained the shore,

Though almost whelmed with waters o'er !

But when they reached the farther bank,

Deep in the treacherous quagmire sank!

And though they toiled with might and main,

Not farther distance could they gain.

Quick to the spongy turf we sprung,

While in the mire the wagon hung;

The horses loosed; with struggling bound,

They gained, at length, the solid ground.

Then quickly to the firmer shore,

With stalwart arms, my brother bore

His cherished, young confiding bride.

A lengthened chain was soon applied,

One end to wagon pole's extreme,

The other to our noble team.

One strong, laborious, earnest strain

They made, nor were their efforts vain!

So sped we on, and ere the sun,

His second journey's course had run,

With old-time former friends we stayed,

To rest, nor farther travel made.

Like warrior hosts, when victory's won,

And present active effort done,

Glad; to their sheltering tents repair,

Where, free from turmoil, strife and care,

Rest and repose may seek the while,

So, gladly found we rest from toil.

———

'Twas harvest time; the ripening fields,

Their golden products fain would yield;

Called loudly for the reaper's aid,

With sickle sharp, or cradle's blade;

And thus it seemed almost a crime,

To idly waste the precious time.

So, as I'd learned with ready will,

In youth to ply with force and skill

Such implements, I paused not long,

But with bared arm and sinews strong,

Engaged, with willing heart and hand,

To gather treasures from the land.

Me, God had blessed with vig'rous health,

And manly frame, more prized than wealth;

And the rich, swelling fields of grain,

Their mute appeals made not in 'vain."

   The feeble, idle, tender bred,

In towns, on pap of luxury fed,

Who never dare the sun's embraces,

That might embrown their dainty faces,

May elevate their handsome noses

At what my truthful tale discloses;

Thinking to one in honored station

All *work* must be a degradation.

With me not thus; the tide of life,

I'd stemmed, with earnest toil and strife,

From early childhood always taught,

By labor, richer life was bought;

And never shunned to work, for fear

The proud effeminates might sneer!

'Tis not the noble, good or wise,

That manly. honest toil despise.

 Time quick sped on; the moon had run

Her course of change, the harvest done;

Meanwhile 'twas noised, the region 'round,

In such a place one might be found,

Who claimed the power and skill to cure

The ills, mankind must else endure;

And while the sun's late summer rays

Earth's bosom bared, with shriveling blaze,

Or equinox autumnal crossed,

Or air was chilled with sudden frost,

While late-turned prairie turf distilled

Its baleful, poisonous gas, and filled

Earth's offspring with malarious breath,

All pregnant with the seeds of death ;

His giant power, disease displayed,

And sturdy manhood prostrate laid.[7]

My skillful aid was welcomed then,

As, like the "Good Samaritan,"

By day or night, through storm or calm,

I flew to apply the healing balm,

And promptly answered every call,

From rich and humble, great and small;

While many homes, afflicted sad,

My earnest efforts rendered glad.

Though my best energies were lent

To heal, not all my time was spent

In this; for neighborhood quite new,

With recent dwellers sparse and few,

(And I an unknown stranger there,)

Could not require my *constant* care.

Thus oft I found a thoughtful hour,

When fond home memories' magic power,

Like ocean-tide, rushed o'er my mind,

And bore me back to friends most kind.

These tender reveries, closely wove,

'Mongst objects of my earlier love,

Expression claimed, or utterance sought,

And song inspired, while thus I wrote :

LINES SUGGESTED BY PARTING WITH MY MOTHER.

A mother's love, what pen can e'er portray,

Or mind its depths, unfathomable, scan ?

Not fleeting, like the sunshine of a day,

Nor waning since our moments first began ;

Not shaken by each adverse wind that blows,
But like the oak, firm-rooted, stronger grows.

I have a mother! Oh, I love to dwell
    On her dear image, though in distant lands!
Fond memory o'er my spirit casts a spell,
    And chains with fetters, soft as silken bands,
My wand'ring thoughts, no more inclined to roam,
And wafts them ever to my childhood's home.

When to that home, I bade a last farewell,
    A mother's arms around my neck were clung;
Oh! who the anguish of that soul can tell?
    While on her feeble accents trembling hung
The heartfelt blessing, lips reluctant gave,
And hope that we shall meet beyond the grave!

Some laugh at tears and think that they betray
    A spirit weak, and are unfit for eyes
Of stern, unyielding man; but who can stay,
    And hear the benediction and the sighs,
Drawn from a fond and doating mother's heart,
And without tears, from that kind mother part?

What other passion is to mortals given

    That melts and purifies the soul like love?

What forms within our breasts the bliss of Heaven,

    So sweet as knowledge that our God above,

Loves all His creatures, and has **made** a rest,

Where we shall be with him forever blest?

At other hours, in thoughtful mood,

The muse's fickle smile I wooed.

An editor, a new found friend,

Sought the unpolished rhymes I penned,

And in his sheet them gladly spread,

By printer's silent, magic aid.

These, with the initials of my name,

Brought neither added wealth nor fame;

For none the unnamed author knew,

Except a friendly chosen few.

I wrote because I loved the exertion,

In leisure hours to find diversion.

The warp and woof, not deep nor strong,

My easy efforts wove in song,

From nature culled by observation,

Or neighbor's friendly conversation;

Or gleaned from not extensive travel,

Required not much of skill to unravel.

    An atheist infidel I met,

And held discourse, in quiet chat,

And there discussed the weighty question,

Which to the following gave suggestion :

INFIDELITY REPROVED.

Who can look out on this bright earth,

And say a God ne'er gave it birth?

Behold harmonious nature's laws,

And then declare no " First Great Cause,"

In these, displays a nice design ;

But that blind *Chance* first drew the line,

Wherein we view the planets roll;

That all which charms the eye or soul—

The ripening fruit, the swelling grain,

The flowers that deck the vale or plain,

The sweeping gale, the gentle breeze,

That roars or whispers through the trees,

And every pleasing object new,

That brightens to our opening view,

Came forth uncalled, without direction;

What reasoning mind, on due reflection,

E'en had we not God's holy word,

Can credit doctrines so absurd?

If *chance* did all, 'twould seem not strange,

If mere *chance*-laws should often *change!*

In yonder blaze stretch forth your arm;

By *chance*, it may be void of harm!

Go strike your head 'gainst yonder rock ;

By *chance*, 'tis soft, and yields no shock !

'Mongst crags, from yonder precipice,

Leap forth ; you're safe, in the abyss !

Plant thistles in your harvest field ;

By *chance*, a crop of wheat they'll yield !

And, if with care, good seed you sow,

By *chance*, it may forget to grow !

Go forth, and some new method try,

To draw the lightning from the sky ;

By *chance*, to wooden poles 'twill yield,

As well as pointed rods of steel !

Enough ! 'tis needless waste of verse,

To fallacies like this rehearse !

But " Who made God ?" the skeptic cries !

And echo " Who made God ?" replies !

Yet, is it not enough to trace

Him in his glorious works and ways?

Then, infidels, in time be wise,

View the harmonious earth and skies;

In all things pleasing to the soul,

See nature's God direct, control!

———

And many other things I wrote,

Which now we will not stop to quote;

Then, patient reader, have no fear,

We shall not spread them all out here;

But turn we now from this digression,

And see how fared our learned profession.

When toward the west my footsteps turn'd,

With eager hope my bosom burned;

And fond desire and earnest aim,

Fortune to win and honored name,

My soul possessed.   On progress bent,

Fired with ambitious zeal, I meant

To tread the path, perform the part,

And tax the " Esculapian art,"

To bring, with power and ample scope,

Fruition to my cherished hope.

Failing in this, I'd have recourse

To other measures, tried resource;

Instruct a school; or with strong hands,

Draw honest wealth from fertile lands.

Except by earnest toil to win

My way, no thought had entered in

My plodding brain; no sudden gain

By startling chance, e'er hoped to obtain;—

Had no far-reaching, trading skill,

Nor magic lamp to grant my will;

Or, if possessed, I did not know it;

Events had never deigned to show it.

A visioned thought, beyond control,

Found lodgment in my inner soul ;

Dear memories, lonely hours beguiled,

Of *her*, who once so sweetly smiled,

A maiden, beauteous, charming, mild ;

Whose lovely form I'd once embraced,

Whose honeyed lips my kiss had pressed,

Whose voice with mine breath'd plighted vow

In earlier years.   Where was she now ?

I knew with parents she had come,

With them to seek a western home ;

But knew not what had been her fate,

Since first they sought the " Prairie State."

Sometimes my fancy deemed her near ;

In whispering breeze, I seemed to hear

Her gentle accents, soft and clear,

Fall sweetly on my listening ear.

Her promised letters, happy source

Of absent lovers' intercourse,

If sent, somehow had been miscarried ;

For aught I knew, she might be married !

Distressing thought ! I'd not believe

Such lovely being could deceive !

Yet, though inquiring search was made,

No answering call the search repaid.

Though in my breast still glowed the fire

Of love enkindled, strong desire,

Where'er my eager efforts turned,

Not further tidings could be learned.

CANTO VI.

A NEW CHARACTER—MARRIAGE—DEATH—THE YOUNG WIDOW.

The lovely heroine of my song,

To whom our noblest strains belong,

In softer notes again we sing,

And to her charms new tribute bring.

Then, gentle muse, breathe sweet and clear

Lays that entrance the listening ear ;

Imbue my pen with liquid light,

While this heart hist'ry I indite !

The halting place her parents chose,

Might be described in plainest prose ;—

But as the shell some value gains

From the choice kernel it contains ;

Or rough, unsightly rocks that hold

Within, rich gems or precious gold ;

Or uncouth seashells claim our care,

Because a pearl's embedded there ;

So this may claim a passing thought,

As here the subtle influence wrought,

Determined, with resistless force.

Our cherished heroine's future course.

A rude log-cabin served to form
Their shelter from the sun and storm;
The prospect fronting southern side,
Was boundless prairie, far and wide;
Behind, in all their stiffness stood
The giant oaks in forest wood;
And all the undressed landscape wild,
In native grandeur bloomed and smiled.

A rough and hardy pioneer,
Some years before, had fashioned here
The cottage; lured by sight of gold,
His claim and cabin all had sold,
And, while another now possessed
The place, he'd pushed still further west;
No spot in view, no settled aim,
Except to pitch another claim.

So oft was done in earlier days;

So oft obtained the choicest place;

And some had thus great wealth amassed,

Woodlands and richest prairies vast.

    To this locality, before,

Some half a dozen years or more,

A hardy. venturous knight had come,

To make this " garden state " his home ;

With just enough of cash in hand,

And business talent at command,

At little price here to secure

The best, and make his fortune sure.

To increase his wealth he labored hard,

And for his toil reaped rich reward.

    His cultured lands of golden grain

Groan with the burden they sustain ;

While numerous tenants till his farms,

His lowing herd the prairie swarms,

And, for his gold to neighbors lent,

Counts full his twenty-five per cent.;

Still, though by all these means he sought

Increase, his dealings all were fraught

With honor; truth and self respect,

His life in all seemed to direct.

Full fifty winters Time had shed

His storms and tempests on his head,

Yet scarce had left a silver thread;

His visage good, active his gait,

His manly form erect and straight;

Yet, while to this ripe age attained,

In single bliss had still remained.

And though the charms of gentler sex

Oftimes his being did perplex;

Though scheming mammas oft had tried

To make him choose perforce a bride,

Looked on his wealth with greedy eyes,

Eager to grasp so rich a prize;

Yet ne'er on one he'd fixed his choice;

Ne'er tasted cup of *wedlock's* joys.

    The rough and uncouth spot where stood

The humble cabin near the wood,

Now soon a different aspect wore,

The soft'ning touch of culture bore.

The raked dead brushwood formed the pyre,

Which, soon devoured, the cleansing fire;

The weeds' and nettles' unchecked power,

Soon yielded ground for garden flower;

And all abroad the space was seen

To wear a richer, lovelier green.

    Within, no less improvement glowed,

And touch of tasteful fingers showed;

Ere long, on " puncheon." floor was laid,

To greet the airy footfall's tread,

With softly blending, varied hue,

The homespun carpet, neat and new ;

The rough-hewn logs that formed the sides,

Bright paper screened, adorned with pride ;

Above, cross-beams and chamber floor,

A kalsomined, new whiteness wore ;

Thus every part with neatness shone,

And new wrought influence smiled to own.

The fairy wand that touched the scene,

Renewed, transformed the whole, Irene

Waved with a magic skill ; her hand

Performed the work her taste had planned.

Though mother dear and sisters kind,

Their efforts lent, and cheerful joined

Their aid, in all thus to renew,

Yet, most to her was credit due.

Irene had reached the summer time

'Of life : the dear delightful prime

Of early womanhood; and here,

All who approached within her sphere,

As Sol, while on his course doth ride,

Attracts the morning mist, or tide

Of ocean Luna's influence feels,

Or magnet draws the willing steel,

Our heroine's beauty thus could move ;

None knew her virtues but to love.

Of course my readers will surmise

That such a peerless, lovely prize,

(Where maidens, virtuous, fresh and rare,

" Like angels' visits, few and far

Between," were found,) could not abide

Secluded, or her luster hide ;

But many an ardent, gallant swain,

Her smiles and favors strove to gain,

Her beauty viewed with ravished sight,

Or, from her tones, drank keen delight;

Some, almost frenzied, bolder growing,

Breathed tales of love, in accents glowing;

While some held more retiring station,

Content with silent admiration;

Alike, on young and old, the spell

With witching power and influence fell.

As the bright sun, secure on high,

Pursues his pathway through the sky,

Nor ever deviates from his course,

Because he wields attractive force;

Or, as the moon straight onward rides,

While swelling ocean's mighty tides;

Or, as the loadstone feels no thrill,

But firm remains, and draws at will ;

So, while Irene all homage gained,

And on her such affection rained,

The surest aim of " boy-god's " dart

Ne'er found a passage to her heart ;

Though ever courteous, kind and good,

Her *heart* " invulnerable stood."

The reason none could access find,

Was, that within her soul enshrined,

Another's image filled the space,

That nought in life might e'er displace.

Though in her breast had 'gan to wane

The light of buoyant hope ; in vain

She looked for word or message dear,

Her lonely, trusting heart to cheer,

From him, who once her path had crossed,

Restored her to kind friends, when lost ;

Whose image all her being filled,

And love her quickened pulses thrilled;

Those plighted ties might not be riven,

That plighted love, so freely given.

But time wore on; still came no word;

Her heart was sick with " hope deferred;"

The knight had all his wealth and lands

Laid at her feet; besought her hand;

Pleaded his suit with zeal and skill;

Promised he e'er would grant, at will,

Her ev'ry wish or slight behest;

Yet, to his ardent prayer, her breast

No answering chord gave back; no thought

Of love returned, his homage brought.

Still, she his offer, frankly made,

In reason's careful balance weighed;

His upright bearing claimed regard;

His ardent love deserved reward ;

And gratitude, akin to love,

Which sympathetic nature moves ·

Toward him who pleads his love thus bold,

Her woman's heart would not withhold.

Her parents also influence lent,

And urged Irene to yield assent ;

His standing high, and wealth portrayed,

The honor that his suit conveyed,

The good that *riches* ever bring,

The pleasures that from plenty spring.

Yet, though they wished compliant course,

Her inclinations would not force.

   Long was the struggle in her soul,

As each, alternate, claimed control ;

A ling'ring love, on mem'ry fed,

That to her inmost life still wed,

Though seeming almost hopeless ; and

The real, present, offered hand,

And wealth abundant, at her will,

Acceptance urged ; she wavered still.

His suit the knight with ardor pressed,

With what result may well be guessed ;

For, when loved woman's heart 's unstrung,

And trembling in the balance hung,

The *present* claimant will prevail,

The present weight will turn the scale !

Dear critic reader, pray don't turn,

Disgusted, and my history spurn !

My heroine's conduct don't abuse,

Because she would not wealth refuse ;

Nor don't, in sympathy and meekness,

Bestow your pity for her weakness—

All such kind feelings are not needed ;

In the same place, you'd do as she did.

So, when such influence all was brought,

Our heroine yielded, as she ought ;

As any sentient mortal would,

Left misty dreams for present good.

The years flew by, with changes fraught,

And fruits of wedded union brought ;

Two infant cherubs, treasures dear,

Bright, active, beautiful and rare,

At length within the household came,

Who gave Irene the hallowed name

Of *mother* ; each her likeness bore,

And as they grew, each, more and more,

Within her heart usurped the place,

Its tendrils clasped with firm embrace.

While thus her cherished offspring filled

Her soul, maternal pulses thrilled;

Her spouse was kind, and fain would grant

Whene'er expressed, her every want;

Joy seemed to fill her being now,

And on her fair and lovely brow,

Contentment sat; and if she felt

Regret within her breast, it dwelt

In silence there, so well concealed,

No outward sign the thought revealed.

Yet, still in visions of the night,

Sometimes would burst upon her sight,

A manly form, met years before,

Once, on that far off distant shore,

Who yet would make his presence known,

And fondly claim her for his own.

Time's ceaseless chariot rolled along

Some half a dozen years; my song

Must now a sadd'ning tale rehearse;

Help me, O muse! in plaintive verse,

While I this cheerless story tell!

Let sorrowing tones my numbers swell!

Behold! look in that peaceful home!

See, what unbidden guest has come,

And revels there! On you couch see

His victim groan, in agony!

Our knight, whose frame there prostrate lies,

By fell disease is claimed a prize!

The scorching fever skims his veins;

His stalwart frame is racked with pains!

His weakened form emaciate shrinks,

The gloating fiend, his life-blood drinks!

Though strong he struggles with the foe,

Yet may not turn the fatal blow!

Resisting effort can't prevail;

The set, glazed eyeball tells the tale !

The soul from earth is passed away ;

The black-plumed monarch claims his prey !

From all his rich possessions here,

From all he held on earth most dear.

He 's passed, to join that numerous band,

In the far, untried spirit land !

While suffering on his couch of pain,

And friends' kind efforts all were vain

To ward the stroke, 't was then Irene,

Like angel visitant was seen,

Keeping unwearied watch beside

His bed ; 't was her soft hand applied

To fevered lips the cooling balm,

The wild delirium strove to calm ;

Smoothed from his brow the matted hair,

The throbbing temples bathed with care ;

Made soft the pillow 'neath his head,

With tempting delicacies fed

His weakened nature; everything

That could the least of comfort bring,

Our heroine's ready skill procured ;

For him, all care and toil endured.

And when the last sad scene was done,

And Death the conquered prize had won,

When duty could no more demand

Strong effort from her willing hand,

Energy failed ; and dark Despair

Meanwhile usurped the throne, and there

Sat brooding on that pale, fair brow ;

And real grief, unknown till now,

In plenteous showers, without control,

Burst from her heavy, burdened soul!

———

But time, the soother of our grief,

Sped on and brought its sure relief;

Still young, now wealthy, we behold,

What graceful sable weeds enfold,

Yet heighten, charms and beauty rare,

And form with Venus might compare;

New smiles have chased away her tears;

Again her cheek carnation wears;

And few, e'en maids, you could descry,

Whose lovely grace with hers might vic.

As honey bees seek fragrant bowers,

In summer time to kiss the flowers;

Or, as the blackbirds throng the plain,

Already ripe with golden grain;

Or, as we see in limpid pool,

The minnows, in a hungry school,

Delicious tidbit dart to seize,

That may their appetite appease;

So, eager thronged the cormorant crew,

The youthful widow's charms to woo.

To sketch them all would prove a task,

Indulgent readers may not ask;

To paint them for your mental view,

Is what a Shakespeare ne'er could do;

So varied were their rank and mien,

If understood, they must be seen.

With self-complacent thoughts imbued,

Calmly Irene her suitors viewed,

Not all unmoved; for though no art,

Or labored effort touched her heart,

Yet earnest homage impress made,

And flattered self-esteem was fed;

And though she gently bade them learn

Their efforts met no kind return,

Yet, pleased their declarations heard,

The assurance of their deep regard.

Though by entreaties all unmoved,

She loved the thought of being loved.

Of all the varied eager band

Of suitors for our heroine's hand,

Few, doubtless, prized herself *alone ;*

And, of the divers legion, none,

By praise, or flattering act or word,

Woke in her breast, responsive chord.

Thus all who would her favor ask,

Their labor found a thankless task,

For all, alike, in answer heard

Nought but the same forbidding word.

In gentle, yet firm uttered tone,

Which needed nought but that alone.

Remote from city's strife and toil,

Its busy din and wild turmoil,

Within her quiet home retired,

With all of comfort heart desired,

She'd almost passed her mourning year,

While infant offspring claimed her care ;

Not *all* of peace, without alloy,

For ofttimes business did annoy ;

Some would the laws' just claims evade,

Others, till forced, no debt had paid ;

Sometimes her darling babes fell ill ;

When, day and night, the mother's skill

Was all employed with patience meek,

Till health bloomed on the sufferer's cheek.

Yet, brave, she all her trials bore,

And had they numbered tenfold more,

Her lofty spirit would not quail ;

Her soul " knew no such word as *fail.*"

Sometimes, when nightly shadows deep,

The drowsy world fast locked in sleep,

A spirit of loneliness would come,

Unbid, within that quiet home,

Which, saddening o'er her soul would steal,

And thoughts of the long past reveal.

Within her heart an aching void,

That much of present bliss destroyed,

She felt; a lingering, yearning love,

That in her soul would rise above

All other thoughts; a youthful flame,

Though smothered long, again its claim

Would fain assert within her breast;

Would not be banished or repressed.

Hopeless it seemed, yet still would stay,

Nor had she power to chase away

The imaged object there portrayed;

The imperious claim would be obeyed.

Though word or line she'd ne'er received,

To base her trust, yet still believed,—

Nay, felt instinctive in her breast,

(The cherished thought her being blessed,)

That sometime, in this earthly vale,

The when or where no power could tell,

The object of that love she'd meet;

With joy, again his presence greet.

CANTO VII.

CHANGE OF LABOR—AND OF PLACE—A MEETING— IRENE.

Some time ago I said my aim

Had been to heal the sick.   I came

To the " Far West" with that intent,

With thought and purpose firmly bent;

And, while the ill my care might need,

To bring relief gave strictest heed;

But later on there came a day,

When fell disease had lost its sway.

Old winter had again appeared,

And frost and snow dominion shared ;

The air miasmal felt their cure,

And by their breath was rendered pure.

The happy dwellers in the town,

And den'zens of the region 'round,

Enjoyed new life, with health restored,

While smiling plenty crowned their board.

Though few at this would dare complain,

It checked at once the doctor's gains,

For his vocation, well we know,

Must thrive alone on others' woe ;

And while the world with health is blest,

He's left alone to pine, distressed ;

Unless, perchance, he has laid up
A competence, soon drains the cup
Of bitter want; and must, perforce,
To live, seek out some new resource.
For me no wealth had been secured,
Hence, other toil must be endured.

With little doubt or hesitation,
I calmly faced the situation,
And sought again to lead the youth,
In ways of science, paths of truth;
For this had been, in days gone by,
My sure resource, then why should I
Now, without struggling effort yield,
And in life's conflict quit the field?

I had an oldtime friend that dwelt
Some score of miles away, who felt
An interest in my welfare, cared

For my success, with whom was shared

My confidence; he wrote me word,

With well-expressed and kind regard,

That in a country school near by,

I confidently might apply

For teacher's place, and thus could earn

A moderate pittance in return

For persevering toil endured;

I applied at once, the place secured.

This, all my former plans deranged;

This, my life's destiny all changed!

From what small acts we oft derive

The turning current of our lives!

Man wisely weaves the web to-day,

To-morrow's winds will sweep away!

Why are our plans thus overthrown?

Why, all our future thus unknown?

The skeptic talks of fate or chance,

The Christian calls it Providence,

More sensibly, that " shapes our ends ;"

And to secure results, thus bends

Our actions; call it what you will,

We all are conscious that a still

Propelling something, unseen Power,

Urges us on to sequence sure,

And guides our will with easy rein,

Whose slightest touch our acts restrain.

Not that our doings as a whole,

Are placed beyond our free control,

For, just as certainly, we know

We've power to stop or power to go;

And, if we stop in doing *right*,

And willfully obstruct the light

Within us, or, in *evil ways*,

Go forward, headlong, all our days,

And sin, with high and outstretched hand,

Against the plain Divine command,

The punishment we must endure ;

A day of retribution 's sure !

Here had I dwelt, as I remember,

From sultry June till " chill November "—

A few short months, yet had I found,

Kind, generous friends did much abound ;

And some, at parting, breathed regret,

Urged that I should not soon forget ;

Regard expressed with kind concern,

And hoped I might again return,

When my brief term should be expended,

And winter's fitful reign was ended.

This, half I promised, still had hope,

With fell disease I yet would cope ;

In practice of my healing skill,

Designed the measure yet to fill ;

From this but transient, slight diversion,

I'd turn with earnest, new exertion.

    Among new friends thus late obtained,

    Among new friends thus late oblained,

One had some previous knowledge gained

About the neighborhood which sought

Me as instructor ; thus he brought

Report : " That in this district dwelt

" A lady, whose bright charms would melt

" A heart, susceptible like mine ;

" In fact, a being most divine,

" That might be classed as best among

" Whom sage has writ or poet sung ;

" And, with her other charms, combined

" Youth, beauty and well cultured mind ;

" And still besides, to crown the whole,

" Had wealth abundant at control.

" She was a *widow*; this he knew;

" The rest, and more, was rumored true."

He charged me then, in humorous vein,

My tender thoughts I must restrain;

Have care lest I should lose my heart,

Or from its best affections part !

I hope kind friends won't think me base,

Or sordid, that I sought this place.

My thoughts were pure, let this suffice;

He proffered me this kind advice,

After their offer had my assent;

When to begin my work I went.

The fortune-hunter all despise,

Who, by deceitful tales or lies,

Or any artifice, would gain

A lady's hand her wealth to obtain ;

And none more heartily than I

Such base and treacherous course would fly ;

And here I assert, on this fair page,

That when this work I did engage, ·

My object was the promised pay ;

No other thought or aim held sway !

Time sped, while Providence had led

Me here to earn my daily bread,

Again, by teaching district school,

And wielding firm the birch and rule ;

To train the young ideas with care,

And patrons' kind regards to share ;

A cordial welcome here I'd found,

And life sustained by " boarding 'round."

At every place, where'er I stayed,

I heard the widow's charms portrayed ;

Her virtue, beauty, wealth and grace,

From every lip commanded praise.

Not *every* lip ; a spiteful few

Would fain withhold the credit due.

None dare her character traduce ;

While to commend few would refuse ;

And these, the observer soon beheld,

Felt envious that she them excelled.

Slight observation every day,

Will plainly demonstrate that they

Who have not wings themselves to bear

Them on the etherial upper air,

Would clip their pinions who may rise,

And drag them to their lower skies.

In this new field of toil I'd spent,

For several weeks the time, intent

On training youth as best I could,

Evil to shun, to grasp the good.

Ere generous fortune, fate, or chance,

My eyes had favored with a glance,

At this fair lady ; yet I felt

No anxious thought, and might have dwelt

Much longer there, quite unconcerned,

And ne'er her fascinations learned,

By personal discernment ; still,

With heart unmoved, nor felt a thrill

Of jealousy my breast annoy,

Or envious pride my peace destroy,

While others, more ambitious, tried

To win her smiles, though oft denied,

And with much zeal their arts applied.

The thought that I should ever wed

A *widow*, ne'er disturbed my head ;

How bright soe'er her charms of face,

Or form, or cultivated grace;

With all her rumored wealth beside,

'Twas all forbid by rebel pride.

And, if I'd felt the wish to try

Her hand to win, what hope had I,

A stranger, without rank or cash?

The thought presumptuous, bold and rash,

I'd not indulged, nor had expected

Success, when others were rejected,

Who'd ventured, without apprehension,

To press importunate attention.

    Of public scandal wholesome dread

I felt, and could not bear it said,

For sordid, selfish ends I'd sought

Her acquaintance; or that wealth had bought

My attentions, or had proved the snare

That lured me on till forced to share,

With others, from their poisoned cup,

The pangs of disappointed hope.

Hence, not the least regard I gave her,

Nor effort made to win her favor.

But, as Time's chariot swift rolled on,

And half my winter's term was gone,

My boarding circuit brought me near,

Where dwelt the youthful widow; here,

I long debated in my mind,

Whether within her home to find

A lodging, or to pass her by;

My *modesty* the first would try;

The last my *gallantry* forbade;

For, in her house a servant maid

And choreboy dwelt, who came to school,

And this, by universal rule,

Afforded all-sufficient cause

To urge me forward without pause.

Yet still I hesitated, till

An incident soon shaped my will,

And gave decision ; this, I say,

My course determined, marked the way.

A dark-eyed child, a little sprite,

All active, beautiful and bright ;

The dearest, daintiest loveliest creature,

Whose smile illumined every feature,

Just at this time to school was sent ;

Whose winning, artless presence lent

A theme for contemplation ; woke anew

Long slumbering fancies ; spoke

In voice that could not fail to impart

To my poor, eager, longing heart,

Sweet recollections of the past,

And opened stores of memory vast,

That thronged my being, welling up,

Kindling again half-smothered hope.

In miniature, this fairy seemed

The vision, that my soul had dreamed

To meet again, on life's broad shore;

The vision met once long before,

And never quite forgot; 'twas told,

This cherub, but four summers old,

The image of her mother bore,

And she the widow's child; no more

I paused, but sent in message, word,

On such a day I'd ask for board,

If quite convenient, at her home;

Responsive message bade me *come*.

   Suspense the period lengthened; hope,

Sustaining, bore my spirits up,

Till the set day; yet doubt and fear

Ofttimes bedimmed the prospect near.

Could it be true, as fancy taught

Belief, that this fair child was brought,

By Providence to lead the way

To the dear altar where still lay,

Impaled by Love's unerring dart,

My waiting, long expectant heart?

Nay, was it true, that gleamed and smiled

Her image through this lovely child?

Was the dear maid whose influence came

Across my soul long since, the same

As this fair widow, charming, young,

On whose loved accents trembling hung

Admiring suppliants?   Were it so,

Would she, the pledge of long ago,

Remember?   Why then had she wed

Another?   Musings thus swift sped

Through my disturbed, uneasy brain,

And rendered every effort vain,

To rest indifferent, while thus thought

My being filled, such fancies wrought.

The appointed day had come at last,

Its duties and vexations past;

The pupils all their tasks had learned,

And to their several homes returned.

The sleepy winter's sun was tired,

His faint, pale rays, almost expired,

Abroad a parting halo shed,

Just ere he made his early bed;

Cast o'er the earth a flickering glare,

Through western forests, bleak and bare.

A quiet half hour's time I took,

To arrange the morrow's copy books;

A moment brushed my coat and hat,

Smoothed down my whiskers and cravat ;

At mirror cast a parting glance,

To see that nought was left askance ;

The school room locked without delay,

And took my unfrequented way,

Where dwelt the attractive charmer ; filled

With hopes and doubts conflicting : thrilled

With thoughts and feelings, strange and new,

Increasing, as I nearer drew ;

Till hastening on as best I could,

When near her door entranced I stood !

　Such music strains as angels sing,

Borne on the soft wind's gentle wing,

Came wafted to my listening ear,

And banished all of doubt and fear.

With senses wrapped, in pensive mood,

With breath all hushed I calmly stood,

And drank in tones, so soft and low,

Sweet memories stirred of "long ago"—

That song and voice my soul swept o'er,

And thrilled me once, long years before;

That song which seraph's might outvie,

Was now her infant's lullaby!

My silent thanks to Heaven arose,

While waiting for her song to close;—

Gently I tapped the outer door,

And heard soft footfalls on the floor,

Approaching; now fond heart be still,

And yield obedience to my will!

  If, sentimental and romantic,

My readers think we now were frantic,

With great displays of *un grand passion*,

Because it is so much the fashion,

That conduct unrestrained must greet

Long parted lovers, when they meet;

That long-pent feeling must outgush,

And each in other's arms must rush,

Regardless all of time and place,

In romance tales; 'twas not the case!

    The door was opened; there we stood,

And calmly each the other viewed!

Each saw a well-remembered face,

Yet did not rush in fond embrace!

Although to meet gave mutual pleasure,

And both might hope we'd found the treasure

So yearned for in the years gone by,

Yet knew not that we might rely

Upon each other's kind regard;

Thus mutual reticence was shared!

So long had intervened the time,

Since met before in youthful prime;

So many changes time had wrought,

That now, when met again, both thought

Our mutual love, we might conceal,

Till future converse should reveal

What our fond hearts had thus estranged ;

What our first purpose thus deranged.

Silent suspense not long restrained ;

Our thoughts and feelings soon regained

That mutual intercourse, which told

Why our first love had grown thus cold;—

Nay, what had caused the untoward blunder

That kept so long our souls asunder.

As oft occurs, the mail and post,

In such mistakes were censured most;

And treach'rous memory also shared

The blame, nor in the account was spared.

Not that we ever could forget

Each other, or cease sad regret,

At the stern fortune that had swept

Away our youthful hopes, and kept

So long our spirits severed ; when

From each, these truths were learned again,

With doubts dispersed, we again declared

A mutual, trusting, deep regard.

   I told her, as I did before,

I had not wealth laid up in store ;

That all the fruits of toil and strife,

The labors of my former life,

To advance my learning, aid had lent,

Was for increase of knowledge spent ;

And though I glad would ask her hand,

Still could not now the boon demand,

By any right, for pledges given

In youth ; yet, would indulgent Heaven,

To grant my wish, incline her heart,

'Twould much of rapt'rous joy impart.

  In sweet response her answer gave

The assurance that my soul would crave;

Though hope, most sanguine, scarce had dared

To expect such trusting, deep regard,

The sweet confession blest the hour,

As dewdrops cheer the thirsty flower.

" My want of wealth she gave no thought,

" Affection not with gold was bought;

" She had enough and glad would share,

" With me its blessings and its care.

" But could I willingly divide,

" (And not conflict with ' reasoning pride,')

" With her, her infants' care ? Her heart

" Said, that from them she could not part!"

  I answered, as may well be guessed,

The honest promptings of my breast :

" Instead of care, her darling treasures

" Would add increase of joy and pleasures ;

" If not, I glad would undertake

" Their culture for their *mother's* sake !

" I'd be to them a guardian kind,

" And help to train their infant mind,

" Through childhood's years and riper youth,

" In paths of rectitude and truth ;

" Believed I could the task fulfill,

" At least my energy and will

" Should be directed to that end,

" With all of skill I might command."

New trust my answer did impart,

And satisfied the mother's heart ;

My words with credit she received ;

My earnest promises believed ;

Nay, felt the sentiments expressed,

Were but the echoes of my breast.

Thus converse sweet had soon revealed

To each the other's heart; concealed

No longer were the smoldering fires

Of mutual love and fond desires!

Her soul that beamed through gentle eyes,

Was mine; I felt was gained the prize

For which I'd labored long and waited;

My patient toil was compensated.

All doubts and fears now risen above,

And happy in each other's love,

Our hearts in sweetest union blended,

Thinking our disappointments ended,

All anxious, hoping soon to greet

The day that should our joy complete;

When winter stern would end his reign,

And Spring her scepter mild regain,

To deck the world anew with flowers,

And revel in her leafy bowers.

My plodding school life would be cast

Aside ; her year of mourning past ;

And then we hoped that nought could ever

Our trusting hearts disturb or sever !

CANTO VIII.

OPPOSITION BAFFLED—WEDDING—AFTER LIFE— CONCLUSION.

In busy country neighborhood,

Where every act becomes the food

For lively gossip, 'twas not long

Before the active, restless throng

Of scandal mongers heard the tale,

Borne on swift wing of breeze or gale,

Or whispered low in listening ear,

That greedily inclined to hear

The fact, whose keeping sore perplexed

Each mind, till mentioned to the next,

By grave and gay, to young and old,

The important story had been told,

That quite too oft the spies had seen

The teacher visit sweet Irene,

The lovely widow ; thus 'twas known,

Of all aspirants, I alone

Found favor.   The vindictive crew

To my destruction quickly flew !⁸

The thought absurd they would not bear,

That I, a reckless stranger, *dare*

To woo and win before their eyes,

The coveted, alluring prize !

   As the sirocco's baleful breath,

All pregnant with the seeds of death,

Its poisonous, withering influence sheds

O'er India's plains—destruction spreads;

Or, as the Upas-poisoned gales

Taint the soft air of Java's vales;

As boiling lava's scorching tide

Spreads desolation far and wide:

As the foul pestilence that wings

Its course, and woe and sorrow brings;

Or as the savage warrior's dart

Strikes deadly poison to the heart;

Like these, nay worse, the poisoned tongue

Of slander wagged ; its venom flung

Abroad ; my reputation made

The target for its fusilade !

   Yet still the slanderers did not dare

To show their hand in open war,

In light of day, or face to face,

But in *her* eyes sought my disgrace !

Like the assassin's sly attack,

Which stealthy stabs its victim's back ;

Or like the incendiary's spark,

Which beggars victims in the dark ;

Thus, in my absence, they essayed

To shake her confidence ; and made

Most desperate efforts to destroy

The favor that I might enjoy !

In such a course was thus designed,

By tales fictitious so to blind

Her eyes, and turn her thoughts aside,

That she should not become my bride !

Yet, though they used the utmost skill,

And showed determined, zealous will,

Her judgment quite they underrated ;

The motives quick were penetrated.

She told me all when I returned—

The day before our wedding.   Burned

With indignation then my soul;

My actions scarce would brook control ;

But gladly would I face the attack,

And hurl the treacherous slander back

Into their very teeth !   Deny

Their uttered falsehoods, and defy

Them aught to prove ; a single fact

That from my honor might detract !

My ire aroused, was quick and keen,

My thoughts were uttered to Irene ;

I told her that I thus would act ;

When she, with that quick woman's tact,

That knows so well its power to assuage

Man's troubled thoughts, and cool his rage,

At once the application made ;.

My ruffled spirits thus allayed!

　　She heard their statements branded lies,

And saw that truth beamed in my eyes;

She read it there in firm expression,

And sweetly breathed the dear confession.

As manna in the wilderness,

Came down the fainting hosts to bless,

Or cooling waters from the spring,

Life to the fevered palate bring,

While listening with delight to hear,

So fell her words upon my ear.

　　" She saw the motives that had led

Them thus to utter what they'd said;

Of all the slanderous tales thus heard,

She had not credited a word;

Believed me honest, true and just,

And in me placed implicit trust;

Nor would she falter in the way

That to the marriage altar lay."

Such loving trust could but impart

A warmer impulse to my heart.

Her confidence I blest and praised,

And felt this trial-test had raised

Her in my estimation; knew

I'd found a gem of brightest hue—

A pearl whose value was untold—

A treasure 'bove the price of gold.

With leaden foot had time crept on;

Winter's relentless sway was gone;

No more his iron hand might clasp

The imprisoned earth in rigid grasp;

The sharp touch of his chilling breath,

No more spread ruin, blight and death;

But spring with gentle scepter reigned,

Her mild dominion had regained,

And troubled Nature ceased her strife,

While nursed again to newer life.

    The landscape wore its loveliest green;

The modest violet peeped between

The tender blades; its fragrant bloom

Impregn'd the breeze with sweet perfume.

The cherry's blossom-laden bough

Was nodding in the sunshine now;

In royal purple crowns upright,

The blossomed lilac met the sight;

Kissed by the dewy morn, its head,

Abroad, its pungent fragrance shed.

The robins chanted loving notes,

Sweet warblings from their mellow throats;

And nature all wore newer life;

And all created objects, rife

With joy and gladness, unrepressed,

Hymned praise, and their Creator blessed.

Fit season, when should join the hands,

In holy wedlock's silken bands,

Of those whose hearts before were joined,

With tendrils clasped and intertwined,

When thoughts aspiring soar above

To Him, whose nature all is love.

'Neath western skies, an April day,

Decked with warm sunshine, bright and gay,

Has more of loveliness than May

Can claim where colder skies look down,

And clouds in frigid grandeur frown.

Here, Winter does not lingering cling,

To chill the "lap of blushing Spring;"

But, though a rigorous power he wields,

Now gracefully the scepter yields;

When the glad earth no more desires

His presence, modestly retires.

   On such an April day as this,

Our wedding day, now crowned with bliss

Our waiting hearts; while lips confessed

The vows, and priest our union blessed!

My sweet Irene, my gentle bride,

Her garb of sable cast aside;

Again, in bridal robes, arrayed

Her lovely form, which well displayed

Her beautiful proportions; there,

(Mantling her brow and cheek so fair,

A modest blush,) the listener heard

The soft, yet firm, decisive word,

That would through life our being join,

And make her mine and wholly mine!

And me the food of envious thought,

For those, her love in vain had sought!

———

Through many years old Time has brought

Us on, and many changes wrought;

His footprints now our features mark,

While silver threads, his handiwork,

Too palpable, our locks display;

The bloom of youth soon fades away!

Much pungent sorrow God has spared

Our lives; yet checkered scenes we've shared.

Our love has now a mellower tone,

Less ardent, and more tranquil grown;

Though burning now with steadier flame

Than first, its warmth is still the same,

Or stronger, lasting, fixed and sure,

That all life's changes will endure.

Though prosperous most our way has been,

Enough of adverse days we've seen,

To make us feel we ever must

In God, alone, place all our trust!

We've learned to hope in Him alone,

Through Christ, His dear, beloved Son!

When earthly joys delusive prove,

Our thoughts will soar to things above.

We're floating down Time's rapid stream—

The past is like a fleeting dream—

A varying landscape—with a gleam

Of sunshine here, and there a shade,

In life's bright horoscope displayed.

With gratitude we bless our lot;

Our hearts give forth no envious thought,

Toward those whose wealth or rank may raise

Them, while on earth, to higher place.

But to great God our prayers we lift,

And thank Him for the precious gift—

Redemption through His only Son,

Who has, o'er Death the victory won !

And while our hearts to Him we raise,

And Father, Son and Spirit praise,

Oh, may His grace in power come down,

And fit us for a Heavenly crown !

CONCLUSION.

Now, farewell, muse; my humble tale is ended,
   And with reluctance we are forced to part ;
Pleasure with labor in my task has blended,
   And softer chords of feeling swelled my heart,
While page on page, my story has extended,
   As Nature prompted utterance, void of art.
And now my work with memories sweet is blest,
Like a loved bantling, petted and caressed.

Reader, if you can find, in this my story,
   A moral, all my toil is well repaid ;
No hope, alluring to renown or glory,
   Has been my prompter in the effort made ;
No wild romance, or high-wrought allegory,
   Has marked my tale ; the simple facts displayed,
With little more, in unpretending style,
And phrase all chaste, with naught that can defile.

The lesson I would have my reader find,

In conning o'er my plain, prosaic verse,

Is this, that Providence is ever kind,

And will our doubts and sorrows all disperse,

So long as we, with constant heart and mind,

Invoke His counsel to direct our course;

He will in pleasant paths our footsteps guide,

And blessings bountiful for us provide.

Another lesson which my tale discloses,

Is one the careful reader can't pass by ;

That oft in pompous wisdom, man proposes

His course, and will on human strength rely,

And though he hopes to tread a path of roses,

God, in his sovereign purposes, will ply

His feet with thorns till forced to turn aside,

And ask his Maker for a truer guide.

APOLOGETIC.

A few words of explanation or apology for the course pursued in the preceding recital, and we have done.

If any think that, in treating the hero of our story, too frequent use is made of the pronoun *I*, and that consequently it appears egotistical, your ideas, in some degree, correspond with those of the writer.

We thought of this objection while pursuing the narrative, but, in accordance with our plan, to present him as speaking in the first person, could not well do otherwise, without making an entire "change of base," and, when the thought had occurred to us, we had proceeded too far to make such radical change desirable.

If you think that the hero, after laboring so long and so hard to obtain an education and profession, should have been carried through, as distinguishing himself in such profession, instead of abandoning it, we have the apology to make, that he chose and studied to prepare himself for this calling only as a means for future livelihood, and not because he loved it. Consequently when the time arrived that his practice was no longer a necessity, it is not strange that he left it for pursuits more congenial. To become distinguished in any avocation requires an enthusiastic love for such calling. We presume, however, that he never, in after life, regretted the time spent, or labor endured, in the pursuit of knowledge.

Some of our lady readers, with an excess of modesty, may condemn the conduct of our heroine, in the boat scene, as being too free and forward on so slight acquaintance. To such we would reply, that she being gifted with that rare quality and instinctive correct judgment of u.en's motives, as exhibited in their faces, saw at once that the stranger's character and purposes were nothing but honorable. Also seeing in his expression and feeling in her own heart that mutual, subtle influence, which, with the rapidity of an electric battery, transmits intelligence between two willing, congenial spirits, we think it not unreasonable that their sentiments or feelings should gush forth in song or expression, free and untrammeled, as the birds warble forth their love notes without restraint or conventionalities. True, we would by no means advise *every* young girl to trust so implicitly in the fair speeches or professions of an entire stranger ; and none, unless they are so fortunate as to possess that intuitive knowledge of character, as did our heroine.

Some may think she did wrong in consenting to her first marriage. When all the circumstances are well considered ; the time that had elapsed since her first romantic betrothal ; the uncertainty as to her first lover's fate or constancy ; the importunity of friends and parents, to say nothing of the influence of wealth, we think an impartial jury will acquit her of all blame in the transaction.

NOTES ON "IRENE."

Note 1, p. 29.

> *The waters had been drawn from Lethe's stream.*

Not used in the sense of death absolutely, but in the more appropriate sense of forgetfulness of the past, because so entirely absorbed in, and entranced with the present.

Note 2, p. 35.

> *I had, I felt within my inmost heart,*
> *Of the world's "scissors" met the other part.*

The sage Dr. Franklin once compared a bachelor to the half of a pair of scissors, good for nothing till the other half was found, and the proper connection made.

Note 3, p. 38.

> *. Due reflection*
> *Convinced me lawyers' morals were the worst.*

With a few honorable exceptions, the line contains, in our opinion, a great deal more "truth than poetry." Yet, because of those few exceptions, we do not wish to condemn, indiscriminately, the whole profession.

Note 4, p. 82.

> *And how much more delay we endured,*
> *While other captain was procured.*

In the spring of 1844, the large, new brig, "Columbia," owned and commanded by Captain Pickering, of Sackett's Harbor, at the foot of Lake Ontario, made her trial trip to Chicago. She had on board, besides her crew, ten cabin and about forty deck passengers, with their household goods, besides other freight. The old wooden locks in Welland Canal, crowded together by the action of frost and incipient decay, had not, at that time, given place to the broader and more substantial stone locks of the present day. Hence, the difficulties encountered in getting his vessel through, the consequent expense incurred by two weeks' delay and extra labor attending it, all so affected the nervous system of Captain P., that he stole away in the night from the vessel while she lay wedged tight in one of the locks; eluding the vigilance of his brother-in-law, who, knowing his infirmity, had attempted to keep a strict surveillance over his actions, and was found in the brushwood not far from the canal, weltering in his blood, with his throat cut from ear to ear, the work of his own hand, that held a razor, the instrument with which the deed was accomplished. The vessel was finally got through the canal, Captain P.'s remains were sent back to Sackett's Harbor, a new captain was procured, and she made the port of Chicago, July 2d, just five weeks from her time of starting.

Note 5, p. 84.

> *But " Blackberry " their utmost powers*
> *Put to the test; etc.*

Blackberry Creek, in Kane county, Illinois. In ordinary seasons, not a rapid stream. The summer of 1844 was noted for its abundance of rain, especially in June and July. Few of the sloughs, (or *slues*, as they were called in the vernacular of the West,) or small streams, were at that time bridged, and continued wet weather rendered traveling not only tedious and laborious, but often hazardous.

Note 6, p. 88.

> *And the rich, swelling fields of grain,*
> *Their mute appeals made not in vain.*

This was before the era of "reaping machines," or "Harvesters," when the old-fashioned sickle and cradle were the only dependence for gathering the rich harvests, and strong, athletic men, with sinews of oak, were at a premium.

Note 7, p. 90.

> *His giant power disease displayed,*
> *And sturdy manhood prostrate laid.*

When this portion of the country was new, and in every neighborhood much "prairie breaking" was done, every year, the miasma arising from the decomposition of prairie sod during the late summer and autumnal months, predisposed the inhabitants to bilious diseases, and one could scarcely, at this season, find a family free from the "shakes," or some worse type of fever.

Note 8, p. 149.

> " *The vindictive crew,*
> *To my destruction quickly flew.*

See " Murray's English Reader," in the fable of " The Bears and the Bees."

> " Alarmed at this, the little crew
> About their ears vindictive flew."
> —*Gay.*